A LOUD WINTER'S NAP

by Katy Hudson

The Tortoise Guide to NAPPING

Curious Fox
a capstone company-publishers for children

First published in 2017 by Curious Fox,
an imprint of Capstone Global Library Limited,
264 Banbury Road, Oxford, OX2 7DY – Registered
company number: 6695582

www.curious-fox.com

Illustrations by Katy Hudson

All characters in this publication are fictitious and any
resemblance to real persons, living or dead, is purely
coincidental.

ISBN 978 1 78202 838 3

21 20 19 18 17
10 9 8 7 6 5 4 3 2 1

A CIP catalogue for this book is available from the
British Library.

Printed and bound in India.

Tortoise had just snuggled in for his long winter nap when ...

TWEEEET!!!

Tweet... Tweet...

Tweet...

Tweet... Tweet!

Tweet...

Tweeet...

DO NOT DISTURB (until Spring)

"Hello there, Tortoise!" chirped Robin. "Would you like to join our singing class?"

"No," grumbled Tortoise. "I was trying to sleep. Tortoises don't like winter."

TORTOISE

ROBI
WINT
SING
CLA

"Why not?" chirped Robin.

EVERY MORNING

Robin's Winter singing class

Robin

"They just don't," said Tortoise. And he packed up and left in search of a quieter home.

Tortoise snuggled down in his new bed. He was just about to close his eyes when ...

DO NOT DISTURB
(until Spring)

Tap... Tap... Tap... TAP... Tap... Tap... TAP! TAP!

"Hiya, Tortoise! Would you like to make some ice sculptures with me?" asked Rabbit.

"No," groaned Tortoise. "I was trying to sleep. Tortoises don't like winter."

"Why not?" asked Rabbit.

"They just don't," said Tortoise. And he packed up again.

Tortoise trudged through the snow and found a new napping spot. Again, Tortoise snuggled down in his new bed.

He was just about to close
his eyes when ...

DO NOT
DISTURB
(until Spring)

"Hey, Tortoise! Would you like to play in our snowball fight?" asked Squirrel.

"No," Tortoise said angrily. "I'm trying to sleep. Tortoises don't like winter."

"Why not?" asked Squirrel.

"They just don't," groaned Tortoise.

"Why would anyone want to stay awake for winter?" grumbled Tortoise.

He was tired and cold and needed to find a quieter place to sleep. Tortoise decided to move to higher ground.

Grown by Rabbit

carrots

Beaver's tools

DO NOT DISTURB
(until Spring)

Again, Tortoise snuggled down in
his new bed. He was just about to
close his eyes when ...

SWISH
SWISH
SWIIISSSSHHH!!!

"Oh, no!" cried Tortoise.

DO NOT DISTURB (until Spring)

"I do NOT like winter," Tortoise said.

Tortoise hiked up a big, snowy hill.

Behind a small tree,
Tortoise found a flat
piece of wood. It was the
perfect place for napping!

He snuggled down in his new bed and
was about to close his eyes when ...

Whooosh

As Tortoise whizzed along,
he couldn't help smiling.

Maybe winter isn't so bad?
he thought.

River

ICE
SKATING

And as he flew off his sledge
and through the air, he
couldn't help giggling.

*Maybe winter is more than
cold and snow?* he thought.

And as he slid across the ice,
he realized he had been wrong.

ÉEEEEE E EE!!!

That night Tortoise skated, slid, and spun with his friends late into the night. He wasn't tired or cold.

ICE SKATING

Maybe some tortoises could
like winter after all.